CLASSICS Illustrated ®

Edgar Allan Poe
MORE STORIES BY POE

essay by
Gregory Feeley

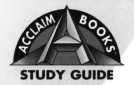

ACCLAIM BOOKS

STUDY GUIDE

More Stories by Poe

adaption by Samuel Willensky
art by Harley M. Griffiths, August M. Froehlich,
Arnold L. Hicks and Gahan Wilson
cover by Jen Marrus

For Classics Illustrated Study Guides
computer recoloring by VanHook Studios
editor: Madeleine Robins
assistant editor: Gregg Sanderson
design: Scott Friedlander

Dale-Chall R.L.: 8.2

ISBN 1-57840-036-8

Acclaim Books, New York, NY
Printed in the United States

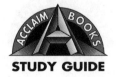

STUDY GUIDE

WITH OTHER CONVICTED MEN, THE PRISONER IS DRIVEN THROUGH THE STREETS...

DEATH TO THE HERETICS!

DEATH TO THEM ALL!

TO THE INQUISITION COURT...

THE DEFENDANT IS ACCUSED OF TREASON AGAINST THE STATE...

AFTER THE TESTIMONY HAS BEEN GIVEN...

THE PRISONER HAS BEEN SENTENCED TO DEATH. RETURN HIM TO TOLEDO PRISON.

WEAKNESS OVERCOMES THE PRISONER...

DISGRACING THE COURT BY FAINTING!

HE MUST BE IMPORTANT TO BE RESERVED FOR THE DUNGEON!

MY HEART STILL BEATS! WHY HAVEN'T THEY KILLED ME WITH THE OTHERS?

OPENING HIS EYES, THE PRISONER DISCOVERS...

I'M IN TOTAL DARKNESS AND THE PLACE SMELLS DAMP! THEY'VE BURIED ME ALIVE!

FEAR DRIVES THE SICK MAN TO ACTION......

IT'S TOO LARGE FOR A TOMB. BUT HOW LARGE IS IT, THEN? HERE IS A WALL AND I'LL MEASURE THE DISTANCE.

TEARING OFF A PIECE OF THE ROBE'S HEM...

I'LL COUNT THE PACES AS I WALK, UNTIL I RETURN TO TOUCH THE RAG.

OH, I FEEL DIZZY AGAIN.

THE PRISONER FAINTS. ONE OF THE CELL WALLS LIFTS...

GIVE HIM THE FOOD NOW.

QUICKLY! HE'S COMING TO!

REGAINING CONSCIOUSNESS, THE PRISONER DISCOVERS THE FOOD...

AH, THAT WAS REFRESHING. NOW, TO CONTINUE MY MEASUREMENT.

HERE'S THE RAG. I'VE COUNTED ONE HUNDRED PACES. NOW TO MEASURE ACROSS THE FLOOR.

AS HE WALKS IN THE DARKNESS, HIS FOOT CATCHES ON THE TORN HEM OF HIS ROBE...

THE PRISONER PARTIALLY FALLS INTO THE PIT...

HAD I TAKEN ONE STEP MORE BEFORE I TRIPPED, I WOULD HAVE FALLEN CLEAR INTO THIS PIT!

A SICKENING STENCH OF DECAY ARISES FROM THE PIT AND THE CONDEMNED MAN RECOILS IN HORROR. THEN, BREAKING OFF A JAGGED PIECE OF STONE, HE DROPS IT INTO THE BLACK ABYSS BELOW...

THE STONE HAS SPED DOWNWARDS FOR TWENTY SECONDS BEFORE IT HIT WATER.

NO MATTER WHAT TORTURES THEY DEVISE, AND WHAT AGONIES I MUST ENDURE, I SHALL NEVER THROW MYSELF INTO THAT PIT.

THE PRISONER CRAWLS ON HANDS AND KNEES TOWARDS THE WALL...

AH, I SEE THEIR FIENDISH PLAN. THEY WANT ME TO PLUNGE INTO IT. THAT'S WHY THEY DIDN'T KILL ME!

FEAR KEEPS THE PRISONER AWAKE MANY HOURS, BUT EVENTUALLY, SLEEP OVERTAKES HIM...

WHY DON'T THEY JUST THROW HIM INTO THE PIT?

THEY WANT HIM TO DESCEND INTO PURGATORY HIMSELF. IF THIS PLAN FAILS, THEY HAVE OTHER TORTURES PREPARED.

AH, HE'S STIRRING!

GREAT! SOON HE'LL AWAKE AND DRINK THE DRUGGED WATER.

A FEW MINUTES LATER, HE AWAKES AND FEELS THE PITCHER OF WATER...

THE DRUG SOON TAKES EFFECT...

A LITTLE TO THE RIGHT. HIS HEART MUST BE PLACED DIRECTLY IN THE THING'S PATH.

WITH THE WALL IN PLACE, THE GUARDS NOW PUT BURNING SULPHUR STICKS INTO A NARROW SLIT RUNNING ACROSS THE BASE OF THE WALL...

YOUR JOBS ARE TO SEE THAT HIS CELL IS NOW ALWAYS LIGHT.

THE CELL IS SMALLER AND HIGHER THAN I IMAGINED. WHAT ARE THOSE QUEER PAINTINGS ON THE WALLS?

AND WHAT IS THAT PAINTING ON THE CEILING?

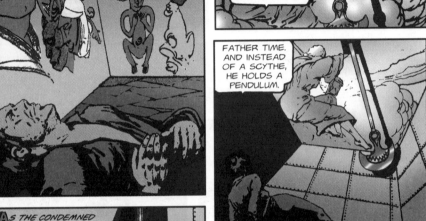

FATHER TIME. AND INSTEAD OF A SCYTHE, HE HOLDS A PENDULUM.

AS THE CONDEMNED MAN WATCHES, THE PENDULUM IS LOWERED A YARD FROM THE CEILING, AND IT BEGINS TO SWING IN AN ARC...

SO, SINCE I ACCIDENTALLY AVOIDED THEIR PIT, MY TORMENTORS HAVE MADE A NEW FORM OF TORTURE FOR ME.

THE FRANTIC PRISONER TURNS AWAY, EXTENDING HIS FREE ARM TO REACH FOR THE BOWL OF FOOD...

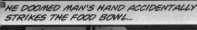
THE DOOMED MAN'S HAND ACCIDENTALLY STRIKES THE FOOD BOWL...

A PLAN OF HOPE FLASHES THROUGH THE PRISONER'S BRAIN...

THE PRISONER RUBS THE PIECE OF MEAT ON THE THONGS THAT BIND HIM...

THE HUNGRY RATS FOLLOW THE SCENT OF FOOD AND...

IT IS A RACE OF TIME...

QUICKLY, FRIEND RODENTS, QUICKLY!

WILL THERE BE TIME? THE LAST THONG IS ABOUT TO BURST, WHILE THE PENDULUM, AT ITS LAST CONTACT, HAS PIERCED THE PRISONER'S SKIN...

THE THONG IS BROKEN: THE PENDULUM IS REACHING FOR THE HEART...

AS THE PENDULUM STRIKES THE PRISONER TWISTS HIS FREED BODY...

NOT A SECOND TOO SOON...

ONCE AGAIN HAVE I DEFEATED THEIR EVIL PLANS!

HIDDEN EYES HAVE SILENTLY BEEN WATCHING THE PRISONER BATTLE FOR LIFE. THE TORMENTORS, SEEING THEMSELVES BEATEN, PREPARE THEIR NEXT MOVE...

HOW THEY MUST HAVE ENJOYED WATCHING MY AGONY!

THE INQUISITORS' NEXT MOVE COMES QUICKLY. BEHIND THE DUNGEON WALLS...

HE'LL SOON PREFER THE COOLNESS OF THE PIT!

AS THE WALLS TURN FIERY RED, THE HEAT BECOMES UNBEARABLE...

UGH! I'M SUFFOCATING.

I'LL ROAST ALIVE BEFORE YOU CAN MAKE ME JUMP INTO THE PIT!

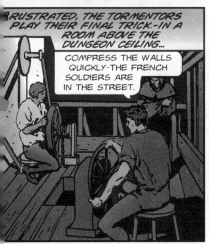

FRUSTRATED, THE TORMENTORS PLAY THEIR FINAL TRICK.-IN A ROOM ABOVE THE DUNGEON CEILING...

COMPRESS THE WALLS QUICKLY-THE FRENCH SOLDIERS ARE IN THE STREET.

WITH A RUMBLING NOISE, THE WALLS CHANGE THEIR POSITIONS...

THE WALLS CONTINUE TO CLOSE IN, MAKING THE CELL SMALLER AND SMALLER...

THE DEMONS KEEP TURNING THE WHEELS AND THE WALLS FLATTEN...

CLOSER AND CLOSER THE BURNING IRON WALLS APPROACH...

I CAN'T STAND IT! THE BURNING METAL IS SEARING MY LUNGS!

THERE IS NOT AN INCH OF FLOOR SPACE LEFT...

MEANWHILE, IN THE ROOF ABOVE THE DUNGEON CEILING...

THE WHEELS ARE QUICKLY REVERSED...

As the walls resume their natural shape...

The prisoner, dizzy, totters on the brink of the pit...

Just in time...

General Lasalle! Thank goodness you've come.

The French have recaptured Toledo. The Inquisition is over.

The END

THE MURDERS IN THE RUE MORGUE

by
EDGAR ALLAN POE

Illustrated by
ARNOLD L. HICKS

BONG BONG BONG

AT THREE O'CLOCK IN THE MORNING, RUE MORGUE WAS USUALLY AT PEACE WITH THE WORLD. THE ONLY SOUNDS TO BREAK THE QUIET WERE FOOTSTEPS OF THE GREAT AMATUER DETECTIVE, DUPIN, AND HIS FRIEND POE. ALL WAS SERENE, BUT TONIGHT... TWO WOMEN WERE TO DIE...BRUTALLY MURDERED! ! !

OUR GAY PARIS IS ASLEEP! SURELY THIS IS THE MOST QUIET CITY IN THE WORLD, LUPIN!

PARIS IS A STRANGE CITY, POE! ONE NEVER KNOWS WHAT MAY HAPPEN NEXT!

SUDDENLY...

WHAT DID I TELL YOU? QUICKLY, POE! THAT'S A WOMAN'S VOICE... SHE MUST BE IN TERRIBLE DANGER!

HELP! DON'T LET HIM KILL ME!!

YOU SEE, PARIS IS QUICK TO AWAKE TO TROUBLE! I HOPE WE'RE NOT TOO LATE!!

SAVE ME!!

THE DOOR IS BOLTED! WE'LL HAVE TO BREAK IT DOWN!!

THIS IS MRS. L'ESPANAYE'S HOUSE! IT HAS A STOUT DOOR! WE'LL HAVE TO GET AN OLD POLE TO USE AS A BATTERING RAM!!

MEONE IS CALLING US FROM THE
URTYARD!

HELLO, UP THERE!!

WHAT IS IT?

WEVE JUST FOUND THE OLD
MRS. L'ESPANAYE!!

HER HEAD HAS BEEN CUT OFF!!

THE BRUTAL BEAST...I SWEAR
THAT I WILL FIND THE MURDERER
AND KILL HIM MYSELF.

AT MAN COULD HAVE COMMITTED
CH A TERRIBLE CRIME?

HIS IS NOT THE WORK OF A
AN! NO HUMAN WOULD HAVE THE
TRENGTH TO PUSH A BODY UP
TO A CHIMNEY!!

ALSO, HIS ONLY ESCAPE WAS
THROUGH THE WINDOW AND
DOWN THE FLAGPOLE! WE
KNOW THE DOORS WERE
LOCKED BECAUSE WE BROKE
THEM DOWN TO GET IN!
THE DISTANCE FROM THE
WINDOW TO THE FLAGPOLE
IS TOO GREAT TO ENABLE
A HUMAN BEING TO
VAULT IT.

YOU SAY THE MURDERER WAS
NOT HUMAN! THEN WHAT WAS HE?

THE MURDERER WAS...

I'M GETTING OUT! THE
POLICE ARE COMING!

"WE WENT TO THE MARKET PLACE AND THE FIRST THING I SAW WAS..."

LOOK AT THAT APE! HE'S A CUTE LITTLE RASCAL! I'LL BUY HIM AND KEEP HIM AS A PET!

"I BOUGHT THE APE AND KEPT HIM WITH ME ON MY TRAVELS! AS TIME PASSED, HE GREW BIGGER AND STRONGER!"

"ONE OF MY SHIPMATES USED TO TEASE THE APE ALL THE TIME! I WARNED HIM TO STAY AWAY BUT HE WOULDN'T LISTEN AND..."

"ONE DAY HE GOT TOO CLOSE!"

HELP!

OHHH! MY LEG IS BROKEN!

JEAN, YOUR PET IS DANGEROUS! TOMORROW WE REACH PARIS. YOU WILL LEAVE THE SHIP AND TAKE THE APE WITH YOU!

"HERE, IN PARIS, I KEPT THE APE CHAINED IN MY ROOM! HE WOULD SIT AND WATCH ME FOR HOURS!"

"LAST NIGHT, WHEN I CAME HOME...

HOW DID YOU BREAK LOOSE? GIVE ME THE RAZOR!

"THE BEAST LAUGHED AT ME AND JUMPED OUT OF THE WINDOW... HE DISAPPEARED!"

THIS IS THE LAST I SAW OF HIM! WHERE IS HE?

MONSIEUR, LAST NIGHT AFTER ESCAPING, YOUR APE WENT TO THE RUE MORGUE WHERE HE KILLED TWO WOMEN! AND HE IS STILL AT LARGE!!

MON DIEU! WE MUST FIND HIM AND KILL HIM QUICKLY BEFORE THERE ARE MORE MURDERS!!

THAT IS EXACTLY WHAT WE PLAN TO DO!!

WE HAD BETTER ARM OURSELVES! WE ARE FIGHTING A DANGEROUS KILLER! LET'S GO!

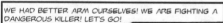

THE APE WILL GO WHERE THERE ARE TREES. WE ARE SURE TO FIND HIM IN BOULOGNE PARK!!

THE FALL OF THE HOUSE OF USHER

By Edgar Allan Poe

THE SIGHT OF THE OLD, DECAYING HOUSE OF USHER WAS HORRIFYING ITSELF, YET I HAD TO ENTER AND BECOME WITNESS TO THE TERRIBLE TRAGEDIES ENACTED WITHIN ITS WALLS...

IT ALL BEGAN WHEN I RECEIVED A LETTER MARKED URGENT...

I AM SICK IN MIND AND BODY. ONLY YOU CAN SAVE ME FROM GOING MAD. YOU WERE MY BOYHOOD FRIEND, SO PLEASE COME. R. USHER.

I OBEYED THE SUMMONS AND SEVERAL EVENINGS LATER...

HOW HORRIBLE LOOKING HIS HOUSE IS!

IS YOUR MASTER IN?

HE NEVER LEAVES THE HOUSE.

COME, THE MASTER IS EXPECTING YOU.

WHAT A STRANGE COLLECTION OF TROPHIES.

THE MASTER IS A STRANGE MAN.

I'M THE FAMILY DOCTOR. IN A HURRY. GOODBYE.

...LOOKED CURIOUSLY AT THE PHYSICIAN WHO SEEMED TO BE IN SUCH A HURRY...

RODERICK USHER! IT'S GOOD TO SEE YOU AFTER ALL THESE YEARS.

WELCOME, MY FRIEND.

I SEE YOU'RE SHOCKED AT THE CHANGE IN ME SINCE CHILDHOOD.

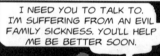

I NEED YOU TO TALK TO. I'M SUFFERING FROM AN EVIL FAMILY SICKNESS. YOU'LL HELP ME BE BETTER SOON.

NO, I'LL NEVER BE BETTER! I'LL GO CRAZY! THIS HOUSE WILL KILL ME, BECAUSE IT'S ALIVE!

DO YOU KNOW THAT BRICKS, PLANTS, WATER CAN SEE AND HEAR LIKE PEOPLE? WELL, THEY'VE COMBINED TO BUILD AN AIR OF POISON IN HERE THAT WILL GET YOU, TOO!

I TRIED TO COMFORT HIM...

I AM NOT AFRAID OF DANGER, OR DEATH, BUT I AM AFRAID OF FEAR!

JUST THEN, SHE WALKED PAST THE OPEN DOOR...

WHO IS SHE?

LADY MADELINE, MY SISTER. THAT'S THE LAST TIME YOU'LL SEE HER ALIVE.

SHE'S DYING OF AN INCURABLE SLEEPING SICKNESS. FOR YEARS SHE'S TRIED TO FIGHT IT OFF, BUT NOW IT'S OVERCOME HER AND SHE'S TAKING TO HER BED. DEATH IS NEAR.

IN THE DAYS THAT FOLLOWED, I TRIED TO CHEER UP MY FRIEND...

HELP ME PAINT, RODERICK.

BAH, EVERYTHING I PAINT TURNS BLACK AND GLOOMY.

YOU STILL WANT TO HEAR ME PLAY AND SING? MY SONGS ARE AS MAD AS I.

SING, RODERICK, IT WILL DO YOU GOOD.

LATE ONE EVENING...

MY SISTER IS DEAD!

USHER TOLD ME HE WANTED TO PRESERVE THE BODY FOR TWO WEEKS SO THAT THE DOCTORS COULD STUDY THE DISEASE...

WE'LL TAKE IT TO ONE OF THE VAULTS IN THE CELLAR.

THE TUNNEL IS COPPER LINED. GUN POWDER USED TO BE STORED IN PART OF THE BASEMENT. THE VAULT ROOM'S COPPER LINED, TOO.

I'D LIKE TO SEE HER FACE.

I'LL UNSCREW THE LID.

SHE LOOKS VERY MUCH LIKE YOU.

WE WERE TWINS.

THE LID WAS RESCREWED AND WE CLOSED THE MASSIVE DOOR...

SHE MUST HAVE SUFFERED TERRIBLY. MAY SHE REST IN PEACE!

...SHER NOW CHANGED FOR THE WORSE. HE EITHER CHARGED THROUGH THE HOUSE LIKE A POISONED CAT, OR STARED FOR HOURS INTO SPACE...

CAN I HELP, RODERICK?

NO.

THERE WERE TIMES I THOUGHT HE WANTED TO TELL ME SOMETHING BUT WAS AFRAID...

THERE'S SOMETHING ON YOUR MIND, OLD BOY. SPEAK UP.

IT'S NOTHING.

AN UNNAMED TERROR WAS BEGINNING TO GRIP ME. ABOUT A WEEK AFTER MADELINE'S DEATH...

THE FURNITURE SEEMS TO BE MOVING!

I HEAR NOISES THAT SEEM TO BE COMING FROM THE VAULT WHERE MADELINE LIES.

...T DRESSED. JUST THEN, THERE WAS A KNOCK ON THE DOOR, AND...

YOU'VE NOT SEEN IT? COME, FOLLOW ME.

LOOK ON THE POND BELOW.

THE WIND WAS HOWLING AND THE SKIES WERE BLACK, BUT THERE WAS NO LIGHTNING AND YET...

DON'T LOOK OUTSIDE. IT'S NOTHING AT ALL.

IT'S JUST DISTANT LIGHTNING, OR MAYBE GASES RISING FROM THE STAGNANT WATER.

TRY TO RELAX. I'LL READ TO YOU FOR A WHILE.

I STARTED READING THE STORY OF ETHELRED, THE KNIGHT...

"AND ETHELRED, SEEING THAT THE HERMIT REFUSED HIM ADMITTANCE, USED HIS MACE AND BROKE DOWN THE DOOR..."

COULD HAVE SWORN THAT JUST THEN, FROM WITHIN THE HOUSE, CAME THE RIPPING AND CRACKING NOISES OF BOARDS BEING SPLINTERED...

I CAN'T TELL IF HE'S HEARD THE NOISES. I'LL CONTINUE READING.

"ETHELRED ENTERED AND INSTEAD OF A HERMIT, FOUND A DRAGON GUARDING A GOLDEN PALACE. HE STRUCK THE SERPENT WHICH GAVE FORTH A WEIRD AND PIERCING SHRIEK..."

I DISTINCTLY HEARD A HORRIBLE SCREAM COMING FROM THE CELLAR. AM I CRAZY, TOO? I MUST READ ON!

"AS ETHELRED REACHED FOR THE SHINING SHIELD HANGING ON THE WALL, IT FELL WITH A CRASH..."

OW, THERE WAS NO MISTAKE. I HEARD A METALLIC, CLANGING ECHO...

USHER, HAVE YOU HEARD THOSE NOISES?

RODERICK! SPEAK TO ME! TELL ME YOU HEARD THOSE NOISES!

HAVE I HEARD THOSE NOISES? I'VE HEARD THEM FOR DAYS, BUT I WAS AFRAID TO SPEAK!

I TELL YOU, MAN, WE'VE BURIED HER ALIVE! I'VE KNOWN IT SINCE I FIRST HEARD HER FEEBLE EFFORTS DAYS AGO!

ETHELRED'S BREAKING THE DOOR WAS HER RENDING OPEN HER COFFIN.

THE DRAGON'S DEATH CRY WAS HER CALLING ME FROM HER COPPERED VAULT.

AND THE CLANGING OF THE SHIELD ON THE METAL FLOOR WAS THE GRATING OF THE IRON HINGES OF HER PRISON.

I BURIED HER ALIVE AND SHE'S COMING TO PUNISH ME

A GUST OF WIND COMING FROM THE CORRIDOR PUSHED OPEN THE DOOR...

AND THERE STOOD MADELINE OF USHER...

AND THEN TOPPLED...

FOR A MOMENT, THE LIVING CORPSE ROCKED ON THE THRESHOLD...

...ND FELL ON HER TERRIFIED BROTHER...

...PULLED HER BODY FROM HIM...

SENSELESS WITH FEAR, RODERICK TRIED TO GET UP...

A SUDDEN PANIC SEIZED ME...

I MUST FLEE!

HE'S DEAD, KILLED BY THE FEAR HE DREADED! POOR FELLOW, HIS HEART GAVE OUT.

I MUST HAVE AIR!

RAN TO THE CAUSEWAY...

SUDDENLY, A BRILLIANT LIGHT SHOT ACROSS MY PATH...

TURNED AROUND...

ONLY TO SEE THE GIANT HOUSE CRUMBLING TO THE GROUND...

THE FALL OF THE HOUSE OF USHER!

HE LOVED HIS SISTER AND HAD DONE NO WRONG, WILLFULLY, YET SHE KILLED HIM THROUGH FEAR.

GOODBYE FOREVER, HOUSE OF USHER

The END

The Raven
by Edgar Allan Poe

Once upon a midnight dreary, while I pondered
    weak and weary
Over many a quaint and curious volume of forgotten lore—
While I nodded, nearly napping, suddenly there came a tapping,
As of some one gently rapping, rapping at my chamber door.
"'Tis some visiter," I muttered, "tapping at my chamber door—
    Only this and nothing more."

Ah, distinctly I remember it was in the bleak December;
And each separate dying ember wrought its ghost upon the floor.

Eagerly I wished the morrow;—vainly I had sought to borrow
From my books surcease of sorrow—sorrow for the lost Lenore—
For the rare and radiant maiden whom the angels named Lenore—
      Nameless *here* for evermore.

And the silken, sad, uncertain
    rustling of each purple curtain
Thrilled me—filled me with
    fantastic terrors never felt before;
So that now, to still the beating
    of my heart, I stood repeating
"'Tis some visiter entreating
    entrance at my chamber door—
Some late visiter entreating
    entrance at my chamber door;—
      This it is and nothing more."

Presently my soul grew stronger; hesitating then no longer,
"Sir," said I, "or Madam, truly your forgiveness I implore;
But the fact is I was napping, and so gently you came rapping,
And so faintly you came tapping, tapping at my chamber door,
That I scarce was sure I heard you"—here I opened wide the door;—
    Darkness there and nothing more.

Deep into that darkness peering, long I stood there wondering,
    fearing,
Doubting, dreaming dreams no mortal ever dared to dream before;
But the silence was unbroken, and the stillness gave no token,
And the only word there spoken was the whispered word, "Lenore!"
This I whispered, and an echo murmured back the word
  "Lenore!"—
    Merely this and nothing more.

Back into the chamber turning,
    all my soul within me burning.
Soon again I heard a tapping somewhat
    louder than before.
"Surely," said I, "surely that is
    something at my window lattice;
Let me see, then, what thereat is,
    and this mystery explore—
Let my heart be still a moment and
    this mystery explore—
        'Tis the wind and nothing more!"

Open here I flung the shutter, when, with many a flirt and flutter
In there stepped a stately Raven of the saintly days of yore.
Not the least obeisance made he; not a minute stopped or stayed he;
But, with mien of lord or lady, perched above my chamber door—
Perched upon a bust of Pallas just above my chamber door—
        Perched and sat, and nothing more.

Then this ebony bird beguiling my sad
    fancy into smiling,
By the grave and stern decorum of the
    countenance it wore,
"Though thy crest be shorn and shaven,
    thou," I said, "art sure no craven,
Ghastly grim and ancient Raven
    wandering from the Nightly shore—
Tell me what thy lordly name is on the
    Night's Plutonian shore!"
        Quoth the Raven, "Nevermore."

Much I marvelled this ungainly fowl to hear discourse so plainly.
Though its answer little meaning—little relevancy bore;
For we cannot help agreeing that no living human being
Ever yet was blessed with seeing bird above his chamber door—
Bird or beast upon the sculptured bust above his chamber door,
  With such name as "Nevermore."

But the Raven, sitting lonely on the placid bust, spoke only
That one word, as if his soul in that one word he did outpour.
Nothing farther than he uttered—not a feather then he fluttered—
Till I scarcely more than muttered "Other friends have flown
  before—
On the morrow *he* will leave me, as my Hopes have flown before."
  Then the bird said "Nevermore."

Startled at the stillness broken by reply so aptly spoken,
"Doubtless," said I, "what it utters is its only stock and store
Caught from some unhappy master whom unmerciful Disaster

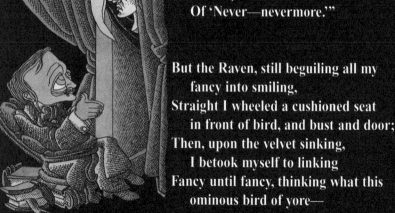

Followed fast and followed faster till
his songs one burden bore—
Till the dirges of his Hope that
melancholy burden bore
  Of 'Never—nevermore.'"

But the Raven, still beguiling all my
  fancy into smiling,
Straight I wheeled a cushioned seat
  in front of bird, and bust and door;
Then, upon the velvet sinking,
  I betook myself to linking
Fancy until fancy, thinking what this
  ominous bird of yore—

What this grim ungainly, ghastly, gaunt, and ominous bird of yore
       Meant in croaking "Nevermore."

This I sat engaged in guessing, but no syllable expressing
To the fowl whose fiery eyes now burned into my bosom's core
This and more I sat divining, with my head at ease reclining
On the cushion's velvet lining that the lamplight gloated o'er,
But whose velvet violet lining with the lamplight gloating o'er,
       She shall press, ah, nevermore!

Then, methought, the air grew denser,
       perfumed from an unseen censer
Swung by Seraphim whose foot-falls tinkled on the tufted floor.
Wretch," I cried, "thy God hath lent thee—by these angels
       he hath sent thee
Respite—respite and nepenthe from thy memories of Lenore;
Quaff, oh quaff this kind nepenthe and forget this lost Lenore!"
       Quoth the Raven "Nevermore."

"Prophet!" said I, "thing of evil!
       prophet still, if bird or devil!—
Whether Tempter sent, or whether
       tempest tossed thee here ashore,
Desolate yet all undaunted, on this
       desert land enchanted—
On this home by Horror haunted—
       tell me truly, I implore—
Is there—*is* there balm in Gilead?—
       tell me—tell me, I implore."
       Quoth the Raven "Nevermore."

"Prophet!" said I, "thing of evil! prophet still, if bird or devil!
By that Heaven that bends above us—by that God we both adore—
Tell this soul with sorrow laden if, within the distant Aidenn
It shall clasp a sainted maiden whom the angels name Lenore
Clasp a rare and radiant maiden whom the angels name Lenore."
　　　　Quoth the Raven "Nevermore."

"Be that word our sign of parting,
　　bird or fiend!" I shrieked, upstarting—
"Get thee back into the tempest and the
　　Night's Plutonian shore!
Leave no black plume as a token of that lie
　　thy soul hath spoken!
Leave my loneliness unbroken!
　　—quit the bust above my door!
Take thy beak from out my heart, and take
　　thy form off from my door!"
　　　　Quoth the Raven "Nevermore."

And the Raven, never flitting, still is sitting, still is sitting
On the pallid bust of Pallas just above my chamber door;
And his eyes have all the seeming of a demon's that is dreaming,
And the lamp-light o'er him streaming throws his shadow
　　on the floor;
And my soul from out that shadow that lies floating on the floor
　　　　Shall be lifted—Nevermore!

MORE STORIES BY POE

EDGAR ALLAN POE

EDGAR ALLAN POE

The Author

Edgar Allan Poe was born on January 19, 1809, in Boston, Massachusetts. His parents were professional actors, a rather disreputable profession in the nineteenth century, and when Poe's mother died before his third birthday, he was brought up by a friend of his mother's family, a tern Scottish tobacco merchant who lived in Richmond, Virginia. Although as an adult he lived in such northern ities as New York and Boston, Poe would lways consider himself nore Southerner than New Englander.

For various reasons—perhaps ecause of the early loss of his moth-r, perhaps because of his Scottish foster ather did not share Edgar's sensitivi-y, perhaps because of the insecurity e apparently felt at being the son of ctors—the young Poe rew to adulthood with a felong behavior problem, vhich often took the form f rash, even self-destruc-ve behavior.

At sixteen Poe became ngaged to Elmira Royster, is childhood sweetheart, espite strong objections from both families. The next year he entered the University of Virginia, but his foster father refused to support him, and he was forced to withdraw a year later for lack of money. He returned home to discover that Elmira's family had been intercepting his letters to him, and had forced her to marry another man.

Devastated, Poe left for Boston, where he attempted to make a living for himself. Finding it impossible for a seventeen-year-old to make a career in literature without a college degree, he entered the army. During this time he published his first volume of poetry, at the age of eighteen.

Two years later Poe resigned from the army and enrolled at West Point for officer training. Although he was popular with his fellow students and excelled in his classes, Poe soon realized that he was not cut out for a military career. When his foster father refused to sign his release papers, Poe intentionally disobeyed orders (mostly by refusing to show up at chapel and roll call) and was expelled. His fellow cadets, however, donated the money that permitted him to publish his second volume of poems. It won him a favorable review from a leading critic, but made him no money.

With no prospects for returning to college or receiving any further assistance from his mother's family, Poe moved to Baltimore, where he lived with his paternal aunt and her eight-year-old daughter Virginia. He submitted five stories for a contest being sponsored by a Philadelphia newspaper. Although none of them won, the newspaper published all five. Though still poor, he was now a published poet and story writer.

A year later, in 1833, Poe submitted stories and poems to another contest, and one of the poems won second place in the poetry competition, while his story, "MS. Found in A Bottle," won the $50 first prize for fiction. At that time this was enough for a family to live on for a few weeks. The next year Poe published a short story in a national magazine, and began to write a series of book reviews, which earned him the nickname "Tomahawk Man" for their cutting wit. Although they helped found his reputation as a brilliant writer, they also made him numerous enemies.

Poe's Work and Influence

Although his career lasted only twenty years, Edgar Allan Poe created a large and varied body of work: his collected writings (which do not count his work as a magazine editor) come to seventeen volumes. (This alone might be enough to rebut the charges that he was a drunkard or drug abuser.) Nearly all his work came in the form of short pieces: poems, stories, articles. He only wrote one novel, *The Narrative of Arthur Gordon Pym*, and only a handful of long stories. Most of his stories are quite short: many of the best are less than ten pages long. Poe's inclination toward brief works is in part a result of his work as a magazine editor (he never worked as a book editor, and had great difficulty persuading book publishers to take an interest in his work), but it also reflects his beliefs in the poetic and symbolic nature of literature: in an era when fiction tended to be long and wordy (the most famous novelist of Poe's day was Charles Dickens, whose books were routinely more than 800 pages long), Poe wanted fiction to aspire to the condition of poetry: every word carefully chosen, their final arrangement formal and concise.

The three stories included here, "The Fall of the House of Usher," "The Murders in the Rue Morgue," and "The Pit and the Pendulum," show three different aspects of Poe's genius. "The Fall of the House of Usher" is a tale of Gothic horror, complete with the decaying castle, the cursed family, and the impending doom that have been conventions for this kind of story since the eighteenth century. "The Murders in the Rue Morgue" is in fact the first detective story ever written! "The Pit and the Pendulum" is an historical story, one of Poe's very few works set in an identifiable historical past.

At this time Poe also began to edit various magazines. Although he was an innovative and respected editor, he was very badly paid, and he continued to live in conditions of near-poverty. The aggravation this caused Poe's naturally nervous temperament drove him to occasional bouts of excessive drinking, which his enemies used to blacken his reputation.

In 1837 the twenty-seven-year-old Poe married his cousin Virginia, shortly before her fourteenth birthday. Neither marriage between first cousins nor marriage to a girl not yet past her mid-teens was terribly unusual for the time. Edgar and Virginia were extremely happy together, but remained poor, and Poe lived in constant anxiety. Nonetheless, he managed to write a steady stream of essays, stories, and poems.

When Virginia was nineteen she became ill with tuberculosis, which left her a near-invalid. The following years, during which Poe wrote many of his most famous works, were marked by extreme poverty and unhappiness. Although he became famous as the author of "The Raven" and various stories, and enjoyed a great reputation in France, he was never free of financial worry. At one point Poe went to Washington in order to be interviewed for a minor position in the administration of President Tyler, but he got drunk and ruined his chances. His own health began to break down, and rumors (almost certainly false) spread of his taking drugs.

In 1847 Virginia died, and Poe fell gravely ill. He eventually recovered, resumed writing, and in 1849 he returned to Richmond, where he met his old love Elmira Royster Shelton, now a widow. They became engaged, and at the end of September Poe returned to New York to set his affairs in order. He stopped in Baltimore, where he evidently engaged in a binge of drinking and collapsed. He died a few days later, at the age of forty.

THE PIT AND THE PENDULUM

"The Pit and the Pendulum," one of Poe's most famous stories, was first published in 1842. A triumph of dramatic suspense, it is told entirely from the viewpoint of the condemned prisoner, who spends almost the whole story in helpless confusion and terror. In dramatizing the tale for Classics Illustrated, the adapter and artist have "opened up" the story slightly: we see the narrator led through the streets; we overhear his tormentors conversing while he is unconscious; and the scenes in which he is in total darkness are (of course) represented by something other than black panels. But the story as Poe wrote it never leaves the narrator's point of view: he knows nothing of what goes on

THE PRISONER IS WEAKENED BY HIS LONG CONFINEMENT...

'TWOULD BE BAD IF HE DIES BEFORE WE REACH THE COURT.

DON'T WORRY, THE PRISON DOCTOR HAS SEEN TO HIS BEING KEPT ALIVE.

The Spanish Inquisition

The unnamed narrator has been condemned to death by the Spanish Inquisition, which terrorized Spain between the late fifteenth and early eighteenth centuries. The charge for which the narrator has been condemned—whether he was a Jew, a Protestant, an atheist, or an accused heretic— is not known. The last lines of the story make it clear that it is set in 1808, when Napoleon's army invaded Spain and disbanded the Inquisition. (It was briefly revived a few times later in the century, but its day was essentially over.) According to historians, the actual use of torture by the Inquisition had ended by the eighteenth century, although adherents continued to press for it, and defendants still dreaded it. In Poe's day, the Roman Catholic Church was widely regarded in America as medieval in spirit and essentially repressive; Poe's readiness to portray the Inquisition as he did is probably a product of this popular prejudice.

GENERAL LASALLE! THANK GOODNESS YOU'VE COME.

THE FRENCH HAVE RECAPTURED TOLEDO. THE INQUISITION IS OVER.

The END

One other detail allows us to date the story: the passing reference to a "galvanic battery." This was the name commonly used for the first electric batteries, in honor of Luigi Galvania, an Italian who discovered the stimulation of animal muscles was electrical in nature. The first electric battery was built in 1800, and various experiments were widely reported in newspapers in the decade that followed. When Poe's narrator states that he "felt every fibre in my frame thrill as if I had touched the wire of a galvanic battery," he is describing the mild electrical shock one can reproduce with a household battery today.

---

while he is asleep, nor what his tormentors intend; and when he gropes about in darkness, the reader is as blind as he is.

This effect is clear from the story's first sentence. "I was sick— sick unto death with that long agony; and when they at length unbound me, and I was permitted to sit, I felt that my senses were leaving me." In the next line the protagonist hears his death sentence pronounced, and after that all the voices merge into "one dreamy indeterminate hum." Within a few more lines, however, first his hearing and then his vision fade away. He is almost unconscious with shock; but when he regains full consciousness, he will be in the darkness of his cell.

Like most of Poe's stories, "The Pit and the Pendulum" is told in the form of a dramatic monologue: not only is it narrated in the first person, but we hear nothing *but* the narrator's voice: there is no dialogue at all. In many of his tales—including *"The Tell-Tale Heart"* and *"The Fall of the House of Usher"*—our reliance upon the narrator's perceptions becomes one of the story's puzzles: if the narrator is so demented that he cannot perceive the truth, then how can the reader tell fact from hallucination? This dilemma—which has puzzled Poe's readers for 150 years—is not a problem with "The Pit and the Pendulum:" although the protagonist has been tormented until he has almost lost his reason, we have no reason to doubt the account he gives us.

The Character of the Prisoner

There is only one character in the story: the narrator. Although he has some interaction with other people—he is condemned by the judges, and in the final paragraph is pulled back from the pit by the hand of General Lasalle—these actions come at the story's very beginning and very end, and form no great part of the actual drama. The narrator's unseen tormentors certainly act upon him: they operate the chamber's terrible machinery, and at one point, when he drops a bit of masonry into the pit, he sees a flash of light overhead as they briefly open a hatch to look down on him. But these interactions are entirely one-sided, and we learn nothing about his captors save for their obvious sadistic impulses.

This one-sidedness is underscored when we realize that there is not a single word of dialogue spoken in the story. The narrator struggles, alone, against a sadistic but completely impersonal threat. This limits our ability to learn much about him: he is plainly of an orderly, methodical nature (he paces out the limits of his cell, making resourceful use of what few tools are available to him) but we know little else. He is frightened nearly the entire time; but we do not know whether he is a naturally tremulous man or a brave one whose spirit has been broken by long mistreatment. "The Pit and the Pendulum" is not, finally, a story about character development; it is a story about horror.

Many famous short stories pit a single individual against a succession of perils—Jack London's "To Light A Fire" and Richard Connell's "The Most Dangerous Game" are good examples—and it is interesting to watch Poe modulate the types of helplessness his protagonist suffers. Although the dominant emotions (helplessness and terror) remain persistent throughout the story, the only change being their steady increase, Poe plays little variations on the *kind* of helplessness.

First (before the story actually begins) the narrator is tied up and forced to stand to hear his death sentence pronounced. With the story's opening lines, he is allowed to sit, but his senses begin to fail him. He loses consciousness at the end of the first paragraph, and when he awakes, he has freedom of movement but is deprived of sight in the total darkness. When he escapes the first trap set by the Inquisitors and fails to fall into the pit, his circumstances change: he can see, but he can't move. And when he escapes the fate of the pendulum, his circumstances change yet again: now he can see and move, but the walls of his chamber first begin to glow with heat, and then begin to contract. This last development is, in fact, perhaps the most terrifying of all. The dimensions of his cell (which the narrator had made such efforts to ascertain) and the location of the pit are the only certainties in his constricted environment; when the chamber begins to change shape—creating the effect, as the narrator is forced toward the center, of making the pit expand to swallow him—the last fixed elements in his universe come unglued.

Character is usually illustrated by action: we learn what a fictional character is like not by simple description, but in the way he (or she) interacts with other characters or with the environment. As there are no other real characters in the story, we see the narrator in his struggle with the two active agents he does encounter: the pit below, and the pendulum above.

The Nature of the Pit
In one sense, the story could easily have been called "The Pit and the Pendulum and the Pit," for the monstrous well (whose contents the narrator has read about, and later glimpses, but never describes for us) returns as a threat after the menace of the pendulum is defeated. Although the horrific image of the swinging blade at the end of the pendulum is what the reader is likeliest to remember, it is the pit that most terrifies the narrator. What is in there?

We know that it is deep, and that it is filled with water, for the narrator hears a fragment of masonry fall for several seconds before it splashes. We know that the narrator had previously heard about the pits, and that he had until now thought the stories about them "fabulous and frivolous"—that is, too horrible to be believed. He later reflects that "Neither

could I forget what I had read of these pits—that the *sudden* extinction of life formed no part of their most horrible plan." We are not sure exactly what is meant by that; presumably the prisoner who fell in such a pit would drown. But we are left with the impression of peculiar horror, the details of which we have not been given.

As the story reaches its climax, the pit yawns again before the terrified narrator. With the heat from the glowing walls causing him to gasp for breath, "the idea of the coolness of the well came over my soul like balm." He rushes to the edge of the pit, but this time the light from the glowing iron walls "illumined its innermost recesses," and the narrator can fully see what lies within. The sentences that follow show the story's greatest emotional extremity:

FATHER TIME, AND INSTEAD OF A SCYTHE, HE HOLDS A PENDULUM.

Yet, for a wild moment, did my spirit refuse to comprehend the meaning of what I saw. At length it forced—it wrestled its way into my soul—it burned itself upon my shuddering reason. —Oh! for a voice to speak!—oh! horror!—oh! any horror but this! With a shriek I rushed from the margin and buried my head in my hands. . .

In other words, we're not going to be told what exactly lies within the monstrous pit. The reader may be justified in feeling some impatience with this hysterical evocation of Gothic clichés. After all the build-

up we have been given, can *anything* live up to the advance billing the interior of the pit has received? In simply assuring us that it is far too horrible for the narrator to express, Poe leaves us with a nineteenth-century convention about "unmentionable horrors" that a modern reader may well find annoying.

Time's Terrible Pendulum

Concerning the pendulum, on the other hand, there is no mystification. Its terror lies not in mystery but in inevitability: the narrator can understand everything about it— indeed, the details of his torment require that he does— but can't do anything to escape it. One of the very few classical allusions in the story can

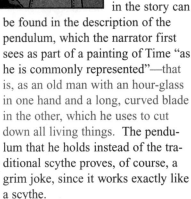

be found in the description of the pendulum, which the narrator first sees as part of a painting of Time "as he is commonly represented"—that is, as an old man with an hour-glass in one hand and a long, curved blade in the other, which he uses to cut down all living things. The pendulum that he holds instead of the traditional scythe proves, of course, a grim joke, since it works exactly like a scythe.

Poe's stories are full of images of time, which is invariably represented as a destroying force. In an early story entitled "A Predicament," the protagonist is nearly decapitated by the "scimitar-like second hand" of a huge clock (a scimitar is a long curved sword, much like a scythe); while the bells in his poem "The Bells" quickly turn from celebrations of happy seasons to a tolling for death, and the old man's heartbeat in *"The Tell-Tale Heart"* is likened to the sound of a watch wrapped in cotton, a comparison that is made just before the old man is smothered to death.

If the swinging pendulum represents the destroying power of Time, it also constitutes a machine, a clockwork mechanism (the clocklike motions of its swing are obvious) that is all the more frightening because its menace is utterly impersonal. Poe emphasizes the mechanistic aspect of the device by referring to it repeatedly as "machinery" or a "hellish machine." Most machines in Poe's work are grotesque or macabre: the device in *"The Man That Was Used Up"* that allows the absurdly injured man to speak; or the inventions of Hans Pfaal, which take him to the Moon but also serve to destroy his creditors. There is one other mechanism in "The Pit and the Pendulum," and that is the machinery that allows the walls to close in on the protagonist at the story's climax. When the machinery is reversed in the final paragraph:

There was a discordant hum of human voices! There was a loud blast as of many trumpets! There was a harsh grating as of a thousand thunders! The fiery walls rushed back!

The imagery seems to come from the Biblical story of the walls of Jericho being destroyed by the blast of Joshua's horn. The forces of mechanism, in other words, are defeated by the powers of faith. Although Poe was a great enthusiast of science (he wrote a sonnet entitled *To Science*, and his stories are filled with details from current scientific research) and a champion of rationalism—as the next story, *"The Murders in the Rue Morge,"* will show—the metaphors and imagery of stories consistently suggest the power of the irrational, the supernatural, or the unknown over the everyday world.

THE MURDERS IN THE RUE MORGUE

"The Murders in the Rue Morgue," which appeared in 1841, was the first of what Poe called his "tales of ratiocination." *Ratiocination*, a word more commonly used in the 19th-century than in the 20th, means the process of logical thought. Poe was proud of his tales of terror, but he felt strongly that the phenomena of the everyday world—the world in which he lived, if not the world he always wrote about—would yield up its secrets to scientific scrutiny and logical deduction. The phrase "tales of ratiocination" never caught on, but we do remember *"The Murders in the Rue Morgue"* as the first of what has become known as the "detective story."

Historical Background

"Rue" is the French word for "street;" the Rue Morgue is the name of a small street in Paris. In France (and several other European countries), one speaks of being "in" a street, rather than "on" it. In addition, "morgue" means the same thing in French as in English: a place where dead bodies are kept waiting for medical examination or burial. So a rough equivalent of the title in everyday English would be "The Murders on Charnel Street."

The story is set in Paris in the recent past: Poe, using a literary convention of the time, refers to the date only as "the spring and part of the summer of 18—." (This convention, a holdover from the eighteenth century, was part of the author's traditional pretense that his story was actually true, and that various details such as date and locale had to be withheld to "protect the innocent.") The narrator is an American or an Englishman, engaged in obscure researches that bring him into contact with Monsieur C. Auguste Dupin, a young man from a once-illustrious family that has lost most of its money. (We never learn the narrator's name; the adapters of the Classics Illustrated version make him Poe himself.) They meet in a library where they are both in search "of the same very rare and remarkable volume," much like the "quaint and curious volume of forgotten lore" that preoccupied the narrator of "The Raven."

ALSO, HIS ONLY ESCAPE WAS THROUGH THE WINDOW AND DOWN THE FLAGPOLE! WE KNOW THE DOORS WERE LOCKED BECAUSE WE BROKE THEM DOWN TO GET IN! THE DISTANCE FROM THE WINDOW TO THE FLAGPOLE IS TOO GREAT TO ENABLE A HUMAN BEING TO VAULT IT.

The Birth of the Detective Story

"The Murders in the Rue Morgue" was not the first story about an unsolved crime, but it was the first to feature a detective (Poe does not actually use the word) as a hero, and it is the first story that details the solution of the crime through superior reasoning power. The first full-length novel to meet these criteria is probably *The Moonstone* by Wilkie Collins, which appeared in 1868. Collins's hero, Sergeant Cuff, is a police officer, and his novel dramatizes the solving of a crime by a law-enforcement official. When Arthur Conan Doyle created Sherlock Holmes in 1887, however, he adopted not the policeman-hero of Collins, but the private ratiocinator of Edgar Allan Poe.

It is striking to note how many details in the Sherlock Holmes stories were first created by Poe. Poe created the device of having the narrator be not the hero himself, but a close friend, of more normal abilities, who reacts to the detective's feats of mental gymnastics with the same astonishment that the reader feels. Poe also created, in August Dupin, the private detective as an unworldly man of private means, a bachelor of quiet manner and refined air. The detective's superiority to the police, and the portrayal of the police as diligent but plodding and without insight, also began with Poe.

The most striking parallel between Dupin and Holmes takes place in the scene immediately before the murder. (This scene, due to its essentially undramatic nature, was not suited to graphic adaptation and has been dropped from the Classics Illustrated version.) The two men are walking through Paris one evening, each lost in his own thoughts, and they have not spoken for fifteen minutes. Suddenly Dupin says: "He is a very little fellow, that's true, and would do better for the *Theatre des Varietes*." The narrator absently replies, "There can be no doubt of that," before realizing that Dupin has essentially read his thoughts. In response to his astonishment, Dupin explains how he had observed his friend, who had stumbled on some loose paving stones several minutes earlier, move from one train of thought to another, which Dupin was able to follow through close observation of his friend's expression, familiarity with his friend's personality, and exposure to the same environment that had acted on the narrator during his walk. This dazzling display of deductive reasoning—a bit too dazzling to be entirely believable—strongly presages the many scenes in which Holmes would astound Dr. Watson by making a brilliant guess based on a few trifling details concerning his appearance.

Plot Analysis

The plots of murder mysteries possess an especially interesting feature: the *real* plot—what the reader most wants to know—has already taken place by the time the story begins, yet is unknown (or only partially known) to us. The outer plot of "The Murders in the Rue Morgue" is the tale of how Dupin solves the mystery of the brutal killings; but the inner plot—the events that constituted the killings—is the interesting one. When the inner plot is finally revealed, the outer plot (and the story) is over.

The details of the murder were presented very differently in the original story than they are in this "Classics Illustrated" version. In Poe's story, the narrator and Dupin read about the murders in the Rue Morgue in a newspaper, and the reader is treated to seven pages of newspaper reportage—longer than the entire texts of "The Tell-Tale Heart" or "The Cask of Amontillado!"—in which the events are described, accounts by several witnesses are given, and so on. In beginning with the actual murder and putting Dupin and the narrator at the scene, the adapters of the Classics Illustrated version make the action more dramatic. (They also simplify many of the details concerning the murders, which involve a large amount of complicated evidence in the original story.) This alteration greatly streamlines the story, but it also has the effect of undermining one of Dupin's most important aspects: he is a man of *ratiocination*, not a man of *action*. While in the present adaptation Dupin is on the scene for both the murder and the final confrontation, in the original story he reads about them in the newspapers.

The story's long final scene—in which Dupin explains about the newspaper advertisement he has taken out and waits with the narrator for the killer ape's owner to appear—offers merely intellectual suspense; the drama comes only when the sailor (who in the story version, actually witnessed the murders) recounts the terrible story of how his orangoutang escaped and went berserk. This would also

"HERE, IN PARIS, I KEPT THE APE CHAINED IN MY ROOM! HE WOULD SIT AND WATCH ME FOR HOURS!"

"LAST NIGHT, WHEN I CAME HOME...

HOW DID YOU BREAK LOOSE? GIVE ME THE RAZOR!

"THE BEAST LAUGHED AT ME AND JUMPED OUT OF THE WINDOW"...HE DISAPPEARED!"

become a standard feature of the detective story: although the details of the crime are known to the reader early on, we only learn the killer's identity after following the detective through the steps of his analysis.

In the story, the fate of the ape is described as a *denouement*—a final resolution of details after the story's climax. The sailor recovers his creature without incident, and eventually sells it to the zoo for a lot of money. This deliberate anticlimax—recounted in a single offhand sentence—could not be adequately dramatized in graphic form, so the present adaptation shows the creature being killed—in fact killed by Dupin himself. While much of the dramatic interest in Poe's story lies in the tension between the horrific killings and Dupin's intellectual investigation into them, the illustrated adaptation must emphasize the plot elements that can be readily dramatized.

Edgar Allan Poe wrote two more stories about Auguste Dupin. "The Mystery of Marie Roget" was another murder mystery, this time based on a real-life story concerning a young woman murdered in New York City (Poe shifted the locale to Paris). It is not considered one of his successful stories, but "The Purloined Letter," the last story of the series, is one of Poe's best. It involves Dupin's efforts to find a stolen letter that has been hidden in an apartment. Dupin's brilliant deduction—that the best place to hide something is in plain sight—is one of Poe's most famous sayings.

THE FALL OF THE HOUSE OF USHER

"The Fall of the House of Usher," published in 1839, is one of Poe's greatest and most famous stories. It is also one of his most baffling and complex, and scholars have debated for decades on its final meaning. Even the simplest issues of

the story—such as, "What exactly is happening?"—are still hotly debated.

Plot Analysis

The plot of "The Fall of the House of Usher," bizarre as it is, seems straightforward enough. The unnamed narrator arrives at the House of Usher, a crumbling mansion in a desolate countryside, after receiving a summons from his old school friend, Roderick Usher. The estate stands above a tarn (a still pool, here much like a moat) that reflects its facade; its bleak appearance includes a small crack that runs from the roof all the way down to the building's foundation.

Roderick Usher is the head of an ancient family, which now consists of only himself and his sister. The narrator is shocked by Roderick's appearance: he looks pale and wasted, and shows "an excessive nervous agitation." Usher describes his malady as "a constitutional and family evil"—that is, a hereditary affliction. When Madeline Usher passes through the far end of the room, Roderick explains that his sister is even more unwell, and is evidently not going to live much longer.

That night the narrator is awakened by Roderick, who comes with the news that his sister has collapsed, and will probably never arise from her bed again. For the next several days the narrator attempts to distract his old friend, and they engage in various artistic pursuits: music, painting, writing. Roderick composes a poem, "The Haunted Palace," which seems to tell the story of his own imminent mental breakdown. He tells the narrator of his scientific theories, which includes one of "the sentience of all vegetable things" (i.e., that all plants possess their own kind of intelligence). Lately, in his mental disorder, this conviction had grown to encompass "the kingdom of inorganization" (that is, of inanimate objects like stones). Indeed, Usher believes that his own house, along with the surrounding decayed trees and the reflecting tarn, has slowly developed a kind of brooding intelligence.

I SEE YOU'RE SHOCKED AT THE CHANGE IN ME SINCE CHILDHOOD.

Soon after this Roderick tells the narrator that Madeline has died, and that he plans to inter her body in one of the vaults beneath the mansion. The narrator accompanies him on this task, and together they venture down into the stifling air of the crypt. Before they screw down the lid of the coffin, the narrator remarks on the resemblance between the dead woman and her brother, and Roderick admits that they were twins. They shut the heavy iron door upon the crypt and return to "the scarcely less gloomy apartments" upstairs.

After this, Roderick's mental condition worsens. One night, during a fierce electrical storm, he comes to the narrator in extreme agitation. He throws open a window, and the two men gaze at the force of the storm, which combines with the swamp gases rising from the landscape to create an eerie and luminous scene. The narrator drags Usher from the window, telling him that such sights are not good for him.

To calm his host, the narrator begins to read to him from an old medieval tale. As he reads about a knight's encounter with a dragon, he imagines that he can hear sounds coming from below their feet. He continues to read, and the descriptions of the fight scenes in the story seem to correspond to more sounds coming from beneath the house. When he looks to Usher, the sick man says that he, too, has heard the sounds. In fact, Usher cries, he has been hearing the sounds for days: *they have buried Madeline while she was still alive.* He has, he claims, been hearing the sounds of his sister struggling in her coffin, but was afraid to speak—and now, she has broken out at last, and is coming up out of the crypt.

In a paroxysm of fear, Roderick cries, "Madman! She stands without"—outside—"the door!" At this point the wind blows open the door, and there stands Madeline Usher, dressed in her funeral robes and covered with blood. She falls in upon her brother, and both crash to the floor dead— Madeline from the effort of freeing herself from her coffin, Roderick

from terror.

As the narrator flees the house, he sees the great crack in the building's facade widen, until the entire building splits down the middle, and the House of Usher collapses into rubble.

What does all this mean? Many readers begin by assuming that what the narrator described all really happened: that Madeline Usher was buried while merely in a coma, and later regained consciousness and broke out of her coffin. Poe was obsessed with the possibility of being buried while still alive—living entombments appear in several of his stories, including "The Premature Burial" and "The Cask of Amontillado"—and perhaps "The Fall of the House of Usher" was merely another of these.

But there are a number of problems with this interpretation. If Madeline Usher had been wasting away, how could she have had the strength to burst out of her coffin? Poe makes clear that the coffin had been screwed shut, and that the door of the crypt was extremely heavy. The crypt, he tells us, was cold and

had very bad air—so little oxygen, in fact, that the torches were barely able to remain lit. Are we really to believe that this wasted woman, after being entombed for many days, could perform these superhuman feats? And even if she had, how do we account for the dramatic collapse of the mansion at the end?

Many of Poe's stories are horrific, but suprisingly few of them actually partake of the supernatural. The loudly beating heart of

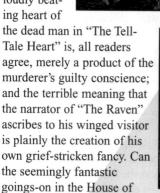

the dead man in "The Tell-Tale Heart" is, all readers agree, merely a product of the murderer's guilty conscience; and the terrible meaning that the narrator of "The Raven" ascribes to his winged visitor is plainly the creation of his own grief-stricken fancy. Can the seemingly fantastic goings-on in the House of Usher also be the product of a fevered imagination?

There is much to suggest that this is the case. Roderick Usher is a deeply disturbed individual, and as he spends weeks in his company, the narrator has, as he acknowledges, "felt creeping upon me, by slow yet certain degrees, the wild influences of his own fantastic yet impressive superstitions." It is during a storm, with its crashes and rumbles outside, that the narrator first begins to think

that he hears sounds in the crypt below, and it is possible that these noises have influenced his suggestible mind. The two men look upon the storm from the open window, and the narrator warns Roderick of the effect of the bad vapors rising from the tarn. (In Poe's day, the gases that rose from swamps were thought to cause delusions and illness.) Significantly, it is only after the air has blown into the room that the men begin to hear (and see) truly strange things.

In the moments before the climax, as the narrator reads from the violent tale of Ethelred and the Dragon, it seems plain that the sounds the narrator and

Roderick appear to be hearing are suggested to them by the story itself. By this time, then, Roderick's mental derangement—aided by the effects of the miasma rising off the tarn—have spread to the narrator as well. It is significant to note that he only "sees" Madeline Usher appear at the door after Roderick has explained to him that she is about to appear.

If there is any question about the objective reality of what happens in the story's final pages, the image of the House of Usher collapsing into the tarn should settle it beyond dispute. Even a decrepit mansion cannot be reduced to rubble by a lightning bolt. There is no natural explanation for the house falling to pieces: if the narrator is not hallucinating it, then he must be seeing something supernatural happening.

If that is indeed the case, then the reader need not wonder how Madeline escaped from her coffin: one can use supernatural forces to explain that, too. But what kind of story does that leave us with? Was Madeline a witch? If she was able to rise from the dead, why did she die in the first place? The supernatural explanation does not seem finally very satisfying. The alternative explanation—that Roderick Usher succumbed to the mental terrors that had long afflicted him, and that his friend the narrator eventually fell prey to them, too—seems much more likely.

Character Analysis

We are told much about the character of Roderick Usher, but very little about the narrator. (About Madeline we learn less still.) If we know anything about the narrator, it is through his relationship with Roderick Usher.

Roderick Usher is a habitually nervous man, although the language Poe uses to convey this—talk of a "family" affliction—tends to hide the fact. Despite his noble status, he shares the same temperament as the protagonists of "The Tell-Tale Heart," "The Cask of Amontillado," "The Pit and the Pendulum," and many other Poe tales. He is also a solitary man:

he has no family, and none of the characters in the Poe stories just mentioned ever mention family members. (Hans Pfall has a family, but leaves it forever early in the story's action.) Although some of Poe's characters possess, like Roderick, a male friend (Dupin is an example), they are all deeply solitary men.

Roderick Usher is also an artist—he paints and performs music, as well as writing and composing. Although none of the other Poe protagonists we have encountered has excelled in the arts, many of them display what may be called artistic sensibilities: Hans Pfall is an inventor and explorer, and Auguste Dupin an investigative genius. None of them

I DISTINCTLY HEARD A HORRIBLE SCREAM COMING FROM THE CELLAR. AM I CRAZY, TOO? I MUST READ ON!

S ETHELRED REACHED FOR THE SHINING SHIELD HANGING ON THE WALL, IT FELL WITH A CRASH..."

works for money, or for other people: although Usher is rich and Pfall is poor, they both labor only at the behest of their personal inspirations.

In fact, in all of his visible traits—his lack of interest in women; his extreme sensitivity to sensory phenonena, his bookishness and retiring nature—Roderick Usher resembles Poe's other important protagonists. The only difference is his mental stability: while August Dupin is exuberant and outgoing, Roderick Usher is (like most of the other Poe figures) retiring, and neurotic—indeed, teetering on the brink of emotional collapse. Otherwise he is a surprisingly typical Poe protagonist.

And the narrator seems, finally, little different from him. They were boyhood friends, and schoolmates: presumably the narrator is also an aristocrat. (Certainly he doesn't seem to have a job to worry about.) Like Usher, he is a dabbler in various artistic pursuits. He seems to have no wife—he never mentions his separation from one—and shows no interest in returning to the outside world. If he differs with Usher in political matters, or matters of personal taste, we never hear of it. He seems to be scarcely different from Usher, save for his greater mental stability.

Perhaps only a solitary figure much like Usher could prove susceptible to the influence of his morbid thoughts and delusions. Were the protagonist substantially unlike Usher, he would have left that unhealthy house long before.

What we know of poor Madeline can barely fill a paragraph. Roderick's twin, she shared his ill health, his home, and (apparently) his preference for solitude. She is startlingly like the two men: had we seen the three of them conversing together, they might have seemed like three versions of the same person.

That person is, of course, Edgar Allan Poe—who fancied himself an aristocrat, knew himself to be a genius, suffered poor health and morbid thoughts throughout his life, and spent his days—like Usher, Dupin, the narrator of "The Raven," and others—among "quaint and curious volumes of forgotten lore." It is not surprising that the secondary characters of Poe's tales—even when, as in "The Murders in the Rue Morge," that character is the narrator—are sketchily presented. Poe was, in the end, not that interested in other people.

The Raven

"The Raven" is perhaps the most famous American poem of the nineteenth century, as familiar (at least in its best-known lines) as "Casey at the Bat." Straight forward in its telling, yet intricate in its rhyme scheme and archaic in its language, Poe's tale of grief and obsession can be understood by a schoolchild, yet continues to intrigue adults.

In his essay "The Philosophy of Composition," Poe explains in detail what he set out to do in "The Raven," and describes how he carefully used such elements as rhythm, variation, and dramatic progression to gain his effects. His essay shows how exacting a craftsman Poe was, but his claim to have composed the poem "with the precision and rigid consequence of a mathematical problem" is undermined by the fact that "The Raven" shares the same obsessive themes—unrelenting grief over a lost beloved, for example—that Poe had returned to throughout his life.

In this poem drenched in gothic mood, Poe finds the time and space to make reference to many Classical people, places, and beings. Here is a list of cameos from "The Raven:" **Pallas**, also known as Athena, the Greek goddess of wisdom; **"The Night's Plutonian Shore,"** the land beyond death, as Pluto was the Greek god of the Underworld; **Seraphim**, a kind of angel, mentioned in **Isaiah** 6:2-6; **Nepenthe**, in Greek mythology, a potion with the power to banish sorrow; **Gilead**, a region east of the Jordon river, frequently mentioned in the Bible, and known for its spices, myrrh, and balm ("Balm in Gilead" is a phrase from **Jeremiah** 8:22, and is a symbol of healing and solace); and **Aidenn**, a variant spelling (and pronunciation) of Eden.

Study Questions

• In "The Pit and the Pendulum," does the narrator feel anything but fear throughout the story? Discuss his shifts of emotion as the action progresses.

• The path of the terrible pendulum would kill the prisoner no matter where it sliced into him, but Poe makes clear that it was aimed at the prisoner's heart. Why is the heart so fascinating to Poe? Compare "The Fall of the House of Usher," "The Tell-Tale Heart" (from the Classics Illustrated *Stories by Poe*), and other stories.

• In "The Murders of the Rue Morgue," why do you think Poe set his story in Paris—a city he knew only through books—rather than in any of the American cities in which he had lived? Would Philadelphia or Baltimore be a less appropriate site for the story?

• Auguste Dupin does not have a job; like the protagonists of "The Cask of Amontillado" and "The Fall of the House of Usher," he is a cultivated European with an independent income. In contrasting Dupin with the diligent but unimaginative members of the Paris police, what is Poe suggesting about the imaginative faculties and everyday work?

• Like "The Murders in the Rue Morgue," "The Fall of the House of Usher" is narrated by someone other than the principal character. In what ways are Dupin and Roderick Usher similar? Do the two stories' narrators also share some characteristics?

• In "The Fall of the House of Usher," Roderick Usher never leaves his house, which in fact shares his name. In what ways does Poe seem to equate *Roderick* Usher with the *House* of Usher? What does the crack running up the front of the building seem to signify?

• How are Madeline and Roderick Usher alike? Try to go beyond the points already mentioned.

• Why is there a crack running up the front of the House of Usher, which the narrator notices as soon as he approaches the mansion?

• In what ways does "The Raven" echo the themes and subjects of "The Fall of the House of Usher?"

• In "The Raven," do you think the narrator's point of view is ironic or darkly horrific? Why? Support your position with examples from the text.

About the Essayist:

Gregory Feeley is an encyclopedist, critic, and novelist, the author of *The Oxygen Barons* (Ace, 1990). His essays have appeared in *The Atlantic Monthly*, *The Washington Post*, and *New York Newsday*.

Quoth the Raven "Nevermore."